The woman who
loved trees

Other books by Joan Maloof:

- Wild Old Woman: A Meta-Memoir from Burning Man to Bhutan

- Treepedia: A Brief Compendium of Arboreal Lore

- The Living Forest: A Visual Journey into the Heart of the Woods

- Nature's Temples: A Natural History of Old-Growth Forests

- Among the Ancients: Adventures in the Eastern Old-Growth Forests

- Teaching the Trees: Lessons from the Forest

The woman who loved trees

An ecological parable

Joan Maloof

1. 地球、植物、動物に深く愛着を持つ者は、その行動のすべてにそれが現れる。
この人は他の生き物を家族のように考え、危害から守ろうとする。
未来の世代のために、今の世代が犠牲を払う必要があるとしても、それを考慮する。
これは、そのような女性、木を愛した女性の物語である。

私は彼女に出会ったのは、自分の人生において富と冒険こそが最高の目標だと思っていた時期だった。世界を気ままに旅し、その旅の話を人々に自慢したいと思っていた時だった。

When someone is deeply attached to the Earth, and all the plants and animals on it, it shows in every action that they do. This person considers other creatures kin and tries to protect them from harm. The needs of future generations are considered, even if it means that some sacrifices must be made in this generation. This is the story of one such woman, the woman who loved trees.

I met her during a time in my life when I thought that fortune and adventure were the highest goals life held. It was a time I wanted to travel the world without a care, and brag of my travels to those who would listen.

2. 私の旅のある区間では、何週間も帆の下で航海していた。

跳ねるイルカや飛ぶ魚たちは良い仲間だったが、長い間海の上にいると、

陸の甘い香り、花の色、鳥のさえずりが恋しくなった。

何週間も魚と缶詰の食料ばかり食べていたので、新鮮な野菜や果物の味も恋しかった。

何よりも、ただ大きな古木の木陰に横たわりたかった。

春が訪れ、私の魂は春のものを求めていた。

ついに、私たちの帆船が陸に近づいたとき、私は喜びのあまり心が踊るのを感じた。

船長が慎重に海から入り江を通って湾へと案内する間、そよ風に乗って陸の香りを感じた。

湾では水が浅くなり、船の揺れも穏やかだった。

私たちの計画は、数時間湾を航行し、その後川を遡って船の最終目的地である桟橋へ向かうことだった。

川の河口に入るとき、私は甲板に身を伸ばした。

On one stretch of my journey I was traveling under sail for weeks. There were many lovely moments; the leaping dolphins and flying fish were good company, but after all that time on the ocean I began to miss the sweet smell of the land, the colors of the flowers, and the sound of bird song. I had been eating nothing but fish and canned food for weeks, so I also missed the flavors of fresh vegetables and fruits. Mostly I wanted just to lie in the shade of a big old tree. It was springtime and my soul craved the things of spring.

When, at last, our sailboat approached land I could feel my heart leap with joyful anticipation. I could smell the land on the breeze while the captain of the ship guided us carefully through the inlet from the ocean into the bay. In the bay the water was shallower, and the motion of the boat was gentler. Our plan was to sail up the bay for a few hours, and then up the river to where the dock, our ship's final destination, was located. As we entered the mouth of the river I stretched out on the deck to enjoy the new

3. 新しい景色を楽しみ、次の刺激的な旅の段階の前にリラックスしようとした。
この先の旅は徒歩で進む予定だった。
私は再び陸に立ち、歩くごとに筋肉が強くなるのを感じたかった。
船上での時間は私の体を弱らせていた。

しかし、進むごとに私の熱意は失われていった。
川を遡るにつれ、空気はそれほど甘く香らなかった。
岸沿いには緑の植物がまったくなく、醜い灰色の建物、高い煙突、大きな円形のタンクが並んでいた。
「燃料精製所だ」と船長が説明した。

悪臭のする空気に私は気分が悪くなった。
さらに悪いことに、狭い川を進むために船のエンジンを始動しなければならなかった。
何週間も清浄な海の空気の中で過ごした後では、船のエンジンや精製所からの有害な煙に特に敏感になっていた。

sights, and to try to relax before the next exciting phase of my journey. The rest of my journey was going to be on foot. I was anxious to be on solid ground again and to feel my muscles growing stronger with every mile I walked. My time on board had weakened me.

My enthusiasm, however, drained with every passing mile. The air upriver did not smell so sweet. Along the shore I could see areas where there were no green plants at all, just ugly gray buildings, tall smokestacks, and huge round tanks.

"Fuel refineries," the captain explained.

The foul air sickened me, and to make things worse we had to start the ship's engine to continue our journey up the narrow river. After weeks in the clean ocean air I was especially sensitive to the unhealthy fumes coming from both our engine and the refinery.

4. 私が気づいた変化は空気だけではなかった。水も変わっていた。
大洋の中央では水は深く暗い青色だったが、とても澄んでいて、
船のそばを泳ぐイルカたちが水面下十フィートの深さにいても見ることができた。
時には、海で最も幻想的な夜に、リン光を放つプランクトンがイルカの体から流れ出し、
彼らが水をすばやく泳ぎ、夜の空へと跳ね上がる様子が見えた。

やがて、私たちの帆船が海と陸が交わる岸に近づくと、水は淡い緑色になり、
さまざまな種類の魚を捕まえることができた。
しかし、水面下を見通すのは難しくなった。
湾に入ると水は茶色がかった緑色に変わったが、
ここ川では水が非常に暗く濁っており、水面下を全く見ることができなかった。

川岸のいくつかの場所では、トラクターやブルドーザーなどの機械が見えた。
そこでは土壌がむき出しになり、私は想像した…。

The air wasn't the only change I noticed; the water had changed as well. In mid-ocean the water was a deep-dark blue; but so clear that I could see the dolphins as they swam alongside our ship, although they were ten feet below the surface. Sometimes, on the most magical of nights at sea, I could see the glow from the phosphorescent plankton streaming off the dolphins' bodies as they swam swiftly through the water and leapt out into the night air. Later, when our sailboat approached the shore where the ocean met the land, the water became a paler green and we were able to catch many different types of fish; however, it was more difficult to see below the surface of the water. In the bay the water became a brownish-green color, but here in the river the water was so dark and cloudy that I couldn't see below the surface at all.

At some places along the river's shoreline I could see machinery such as tractors and bulldozers. In those areas the soil was exposed, and I imagined

5. 雨が降ると、土壌が川に流れ込み、水が濁る原因
になっていた。

川岸の他の場所では、まだ木々が残っていたが、奇
妙なことにすべて同じ種類の木であり、
世界の他の森で見たような多様な木々の混在はなか
った。
川を遡るにつれて、ある場所では木が伐採され、切
り株と雑草だけが残っていた。
それらの地域は暑く荒れ果てた印象を受けた。
時折、伐採された場所の中央で、大量の枝が積み上
げられ、煙を上げて燃えていた。
煙にさらされるのは久しぶりだったため、私は驚く
ほど敏感になっていた。
煙は私の目と喉に焼けるような痛みを引き起こした
。

ある地点を通過したとき、その匂いは特に不快だっ
たが、私はそれが何なのかわからなかった。
「下水処理場だ」と船長が私の無言の疑問に答えた
。
「下水が...」。

that during rainstorms the soil washed into the river and caused its cloudiness.

In other places along the shoreline I could see that there were still trees but, strangely, they were all the same kind, not a mixture of trees as I had seen in other forests of the world. As we continued upriver I noticed that in some places the trees had been cut down and all that remained were stumps and weeds. Those areas looked hot and barren to me. Sometimes there was smoke coming off big piles of branches in the middle of the cleared areas. It had been a long while since I had been exposed to smoke, and I was surprisingly sensitive to it. The smoke caused a burning feeling in my eyes and throat.

At one location we passed, the smell was particularly unpleasant, but I could not determine what it was.

"Sewage treatment plant," the captain replied to my unspoken question. "After the sewage

6. 処理施設を通過した後、下水は川へと流れ出る
。
時には施設が正常に機能せず、下水がそのまま川
に流れ込むこともある。

その川の魚を食べることを考えると気分が悪くな
ったが、
船上には他に食料がなく、すでに昼食の時間を過
ぎていた。
私たちは濁った茶色の水に釣り糸を垂らしたが、
一時間経っても何も釣れず、ついに諦めた。

桟橋に到着した時には、私はほとんど空腹で力尽
きそうだった。
荷物をまとめ、船長と最後の会話を交わし、別れ
を告げた。
再び彼に会うことがあるのか、私は知る由もなか
った。

長い間船上にいたせいで、大地は足元で奇妙に感
じられた。
揺れ動くように感じ、しっかりとした地面とはま
るで違っていた…。

goes through the treatment plant it flows out into the river. Sometimes the plant doesn't work right, and the sewage just goes straight into the river."

The thought of eating fish out of that river was nauseating to me, but we had no other food left on board, and it was past time for our mid-day meal. We cast our lines into that murky brownness, but we gave up after an hour of fishing and not catching anything.

By the time we reached the dock I was almost weak from hunger. I gathered my belongings together, had a last conversation with the captain, and bid him farewell - not knowing if I would ever see him again.

After all that time on board ship the land felt strange beneath my feet; it seemed to sway and rock, it was nothing like the solid ground I remembered.

7. 私は思い出した。陸に上がった最初の目的は食べ
物を手に入れることだった。
近くの別の船にいた紳士に声をかけ、もしかすると
彼は釣りの運が良く、
私に何かを売ってくれるかもしれないと思った。
何週間ぶりかに違う顔を見るのは奇妙な感じだった
。
「魚は食えんよ」と彼は荒々しく言った。
「水銀が入ってる。上流の工場からか、下水処理場
からか、それとも
二十年前の流出事故のせいか分からんがな。保健所
が食べるなって言ってる。」
この状況は私にとって悲しくも奇妙だったが、正直
なところ、しばらく魚を食べなくても構わなかった
その老人は道を指し示し、「そこに食事ができる場
所がある」と教えてくれた。
私はリュックを背負い、ふらつく足取りで道を歩き
始めた。
道は舗装されており、その脇には狭い歩道があった
。
車が猛スピードで近くを走り抜けるのは恐ろしかっ
た。
すると、一台の車から誰かが燃えたタバコの吸い殻
を投げ捨てた。

My first goal on land was to get some food. I approached a gentleman on another nearby boat - thinking that perhaps he had had better luck with his fishing and would be willing to sell me something. It was odd to see a different face after all those weeks.

"Can't eat the fish," he gruffed back. "Mercury. Don't know if it's coming from the factory upriver a ways, the sewage treatment plant, or the spill we had here twenty years back. Health Department says we can't eat it."

This was a sad and strange situation to me, but if truth be told I was just as happy not to eat fish for a while. The old gentleman directed me up the road where he said there was a place to eat. I lifted my pack and started my first wobbly steps down the road. The road was paved and there was a narrow area off to the side where I could walk. It was frightening to have cars speeding by so closely. Out of one car someone threw a burning cigarette butt.

8.　ついに私はレストランに到着した。
建物の周囲はアスファルトで覆われ、車をすぐ近く
に停めることができた。
屋根はプラスチックのような見た目だった。
中に入ると、消毒剤と油の混ざった匂いがした。
もし空腹でなければ、すぐに引き返しただろう。

店内は非常に明るく、蛍光灯が何列も並んでいた。
長い間、蛍光灯の光を見ていなかったことに気づい
た。
店の中の人々はほとんどが太っていて、新品のよう
な、明るい色や派手な模様の服を着ていた。
その明るい光の下では、彼らはまるで道化師のよう
に見えた。
多くの子供たちが親と口論していた。

私はまばたきを繰り返し、頭がくらくらしながらカ
ウンターへ向かった。
新鮮な野菜があるか尋ねた。

「ありません。」

果物は？

「ありません。」

困惑しながら、私はメニューの最初のものを注文し
た...。

At last I came to the restaurant; it was surrounded by asphalt, so people could park their cars up close to the building, and it had a plastic looking roof. Inside, it smelled like disinfectant and grease. If I weren't so hungry I would have turned around and left. The inside was very bright, with rows and rows of fluorescent lights; I realized it had been a long time since I'd seen fluorescent lighting. The people inside were almost all overweight, and they were wearing clothes that looked very new, with very bright colors and patterns. The bright lights made them look like clowns to me. Many of the children were arguing with their parents. My eyes were blinking, and my head was spinning as I stepped to the counter to order. I asked what kind of fresh vegetables they had.

"None."

Fruits?

"None."

Confused, I just ordered the first thing on

9. リストにあったものを注文したが、店内の匂いそ
のままの味がした。
しかし、空腹は満たされた。
もう腹は減っていなかったので、私は再び道を進ん
だ。
一マイルほど歩いた後、胃に奇妙な重い感覚を覚え
た。
食べたもののせいかもしれないし、単に神経のせい
かもしれなかった。

私は再び川へ向かった。
私の計画は、川沿いを歩いて国の内陸へ進むことだ
った。
しかし、桟橋に戻り川沿いの道を探してみると、
そこには進路をふさぐフェンスがあるだけだった。
フェンスの向こうには、短い緑の芝生に囲まれた家
があった。
家の外には、子供が遊ぶ場所、屋外で料理をする場
所、
そしてテーブルと椅子など、さまざまなものが置か
れていた。
そのテーブルに座ってしばらく休みたかったが、そ
こが私有地であることは明らかだった。

フェンスに囲まれた庭の向こうには、同じくフェン
スに囲まれた別の家があり、
同様のものが庭に並んでいた。
どちらの方向にも、歩行者が川にアクセスできる場
所はなかった。
反対側の川岸も同じような状況のように見えた。
最終的に私は引き返さざるを得ないことを悟った…。

the list; it tasted like the place smelled, but it did fill me up. No longer hungry, I continued down the road. After walking about a mile I got a strange heavy feeling in my stomach. I suspected that it was from the food, but it could have been my nerves.

I headed back toward the river. My plan was to follow the river, on foot, up into the interior of the country, but when I got back to the dock and looked for a path along the river all I found was a fence that blocked my way. Behind the fence was a house surrounded by short green grass. There were numerous objects outside of the house, such as a place for children to play, a place for cooking outdoors, and a table and chairs. I would have loved to sit at that table for a time to collect myself, but I could tell that it was a private place. Beyond the fenced-in yard was another house with a fenced-in yard and similar items outside. In both directions access to the river was cut off from walkers, and it appeared to be the same situation on the other side of the river. Eventually I realized that I had to turn

10. 引き返し、レストランへ向かう道を再び歩き始め
た。

再びレストランの前を通ると、そこはまだ奇妙な人
々で満員だった。
私が歩いている道路は次第に大きくなり、車の数も
増え、速度も上がっていた。
私はこの土地を歩いて横断しようとする自分の決意
を疑い始めた。
歩いている人は他におらず、車の中の人々が私をじ
っと見つめているのが不快だった。
私は無防備でさらされているように感じ、日陰もほ
とんどなかった。
田舎へ続く道を切望したが、すべてがフェンスで囲
まれ、
「私有地」と掲示されていた。
これほど広大な国にいるのに、
私の足跡がこの狭い道路沿いの一筋に制限されてい
るのは奇妙に思えた。

最初の日の終わりに、雨が降り始めた。
道が交差する場所があり、その下は雨をしのぐこと
ができた。
私は平らな場所を見つけ、そこで休むことにした…。

around and head back down the road toward the restaurant.

I passed the restaurant again and it was still full of strange looking people. The road I was walking along became larger and the cars more numerous and faster. I was beginning to question my desire to walk across this land. I didn't see anyone else walking, and it was uncomfortable to have everyone in the cars staring at me. I felt exposed and vulnerable and there was very little shade. I longed for a path that would take me into the countryside, but everything was fenced, or posted as private property. It was a very large country that I was in, so it seemed strange to me that my footsteps were restricted to a very narrow strip along the road.

At the end of the first day it started to rain. There was a place where one road crossed over top another, and underneath I was sheltered from the rain. I found a flat spot to make a resting place, and

11. 車が猛スピードで通り過ぎる音を聞きながら眠り
についた。
それはとても奇妙な一日だった。

真夜中、長髪で無精ひげの男が現れた。
彼は大声で話しており、その声で私は目を覚ました
。
見知らぬ男に私は怯えた。
最初は私に話しかけているのかと思ったが、
しばらくすると彼は独り言を言っているか、
架空の誰かと話しているのだと気づいた。
しばらく耳を傾けたが、彼が何を言っているのか理
解できなかった。
そもそも彼が私の存在に気づいていたのかさえ分か
らなかった。
彼もまた平らな場所を見つけて横になり眠りについ
たが、
彼の頻繁な咳が私たち二人の眠りを妨げた。

朝早く、男が目を覚ます前に、私は道を進み続けた
。
しかしその日、私は道端で一人ではなかった。
車道と出会う私道のところどころに、子供が一人、
または子供たちのグループが見えた。
大人と一緒にいることもあれば、いないこともあっ
た。
彼らはどこかへ歩いて行くわけではなく、ただ立っ
て待っていた

fell asleep to the sound of cars whizzing by. It had been a very unusual day.

In the middle of the night a man with long hair and a stubbly beard appeared. He was talking loudly, and his talking woke me. I was frightened by the stranger. At first I thought he was talking to me, but after a while I realized that he was talking to himself, or to some imaginary person. I listened for a time, but I could not understand what he was saying. I'm not even sure if he was aware of my presence. He too found a flat spot to lie down and sleep; but his frequent coughing disturbed both of us throughout the night.

Early in the morning, before the man woke up, I continued down the road. On that day, however, I was not alone on the roadside. Every so often, where a driveway met the road, I could see a child, or a group of children, sometimes with adults, sometimes without. They were not walking anywhere; they were just standing and waiting. It

12. 朝はとても早く、子供たちのほとんどは寝起きの
ような顔をしていた。
彼らは道路脇に立つより、ベッドに戻りたそうに見
えた。
私がその子供たちのグループの横を通り過ぎると、
大きな黄色いバスが停まり、
子供たちは中に乗り込んだ。
彼らは学校へ向かうのだった。

その日一日、道路は再び人影が消えた。
車の外にいる人はほとんどいなかった。
私はまた、あのプラスチックの屋根の店で食事を取
ることになった。
そこしか開いている店がなかったのだ。
徒歩の長い旅になることを願っていたが、すでに自
分の計画に疑問を抱き始めていた。
この道路沿いの歩行はまったく楽しくなかった。

しかし、すぐに諦めるのではなく、計画を調整する
ことにした。
特定の方向を目指すのではなく、出会った最も小さ
な道を選ぶことにした。
それがどの方向へ向かっていようとも。
数マイル進んだところで、今歩いている道よりもさ
らに小さな道を見つけたので、そちらへ曲がった。

新しい道は交通量が少なかったが…。

was very early and most of them had that just-woken-up look. They looked like they would rather be back in bed than standing beside the road. As I passed one of these groups a big yellow bus stopped and the children got inside. They were going to school.

For the rest of the day the roads were empty of people again, people outside of cars that is. I had to eat at another one of those plastic-roofed places because it was the only thing I passed that was open. It was the second day of what I hoped would be a long journey by foot, but already I doubted my plan. This roadside walking was no fun.

Rather than give up so soon, I decided to adjust my plan. Instead of heading in a particular direction I would just take the smallest road I came across, no matter what direction it was headed in. After a few miles I came to a road smaller than the one I was walking along; so I turned down it.

The new road had much less traffic, but the

13 道沿いには何マイルも続く農地しかなかった。
せめて果物や野菜が手に入るかと思ったが、
見渡す限りの畑は若いトウモロコシや大豆の苗ばかりだった。
ある畑では、大きなトラクターが奇妙な化学臭のする液体を散布していた。
私は息を止めてその畑のそばを歩いたが、畑があまりにも広く、
臭いを通り過ぎる前に息をしなければならなかった。

時々、道路脇に死んだ動物を見かけた。
ある日、新しく車に轢かれたと思われるウサギを通り過ぎ、
その半マイル後には、ハエにたかられ、数日経ったようなアライグマの死体を目にした。
踏み潰されたカエルは数えきれないほどだった。

太陽が空の低い位置に傾き始めると、今夜どこで眠るのか考え始めた。
ちょうどその時、私は誰かの私道のそばを歩いていた。
その家の女性が郵便受けから今日の郵便を取りに出てきた。
私は思い切って、どこか眠れる場所を知らないか尋ねてみることにした。
驚いたことに、その親切な女性は私に...。

only thing along it was farm fields for miles and miles. Maybe now I could at least get some fruits and vegetables I thought, but field after field was either young corn plants or soybean seedlings. In one field there was a very large tractor spraying a liquid with a strange chemical smell. I tried to hold my breath as I walked by that field, but the field was too large, and I had to start breathing again before I got past the smell. Occasionally I had to walk by dead animals on the roadside. One day I passed a rabbit that looked like it had been freshly killed, by a car no doubt, and a half mile later I had to walk by a raccoon that was covered with flies and smelled like it had been there a few days. There were too many squashed frogs to count.

When the sun started getting low in the sky I began to wonder about where I would sleep that night. Coincidentally, I was walking by someone's driveway when a woman walked out to her roadside mailbox to pick up the day's mail. I decided to take a chance and ask if she knew of a place I could sleep. Incredibly, this kind woman offered me, a

14. 見知らぬ私に、彼女は寝る場所を提供してくれた
私は彼女のポーチへと招かれた。

「お腹が空いているでしょう？」と彼女は言った。

その通りだった。最後の食事から長い時間が経って
いた。
彼女はポーチにポテトチップスの入ったボウルと冷
たいソーダを持ってきてくれた。
私は彼女の親切に甘え、それを食べ飲んだ。

「チャーリーに電話して、ピザをもう一枚持ってき
てもらうわ。
今夜はピザパレスで、たった二ドル追加すればもう
一枚手に入るのよ。」

彼女が何の話をしているのか完全には理解できなか
ったが、
長い時間を一人で過ごした後だったので、
女性の優しい話し相手がいることがありがたかった
。
彼女はとても親切で寛大だったが、
目を逸らさなければならないような独特の外見的特
徴を持っていた。
まず、彼女は非常に大柄な女性だったが、
彼女の服はどれも体に対して小さすぎるように見え
た。
彼女のズボンはターコイズブルーで、靴と同じ色を
していた。
しかし、膝下までしかなく、歩くたびにこすれる音
がした。
彼女の靴は小さな鋭いヒールがあり、彼女の足は…。

stranger, a place to sleep. I was invited up to her porch.

"You must be hungry," she said.

And she was right; it had been a long time since my last meal. Out to the porch she brought a bowl of potato chips and a cold soda. I ate and drank what the kind woman offered.

"I'll call Charlie and get him to pick up an extra pizza," she said, "for only two dollars more you can get a second one at the Pizza Palace tonight."

I wasn't quite sure what she was talking about, but I was grateful for some female companionship after all that time. Although she was very friendly, and very generous, she had some interesting physical characteristics that I had to keep from staring at. To begin with she was a very large woman, but her clothes all seemed too small for her. Her pants were a turquoise blue - the same color as her shoes - but they only went to just below her knees, and they made a rubbing sound when she walked. Her shoes had little sharp heels and her feet

15. 彼女の体は服からはみ出しそうだった。
彼女の指と足の爪は明るいピンクがかったバラ色に
塗られていた。
髪はほとんどが淡い黄色だったが、頭に近い部分は
濃い茶色だった。
私の母と同じくらいの年齢なのかもしれない。

チップスを食べ終わると、私たちは家の中に入り、
テレビを見た。
テレビを見るのは本当に久しぶりだった。
チャーリーは暗くなってからずっと後に帰ってきた
。
彼はとても疲れているように見え、私に会えて特に
嬉しそうではなかった。
しかし、それでも私たちはテレビの前で一緒にピザ
を食べた。
わずかな会話から、彼が一日中、誰かに与えられた
仕事をこなしていたのだと察した。
一時間ほどテレビを見た後、チャーリーは寝ると言
い、私は寝室へ案内された。

私の部屋のベッドにはぬいぐるみがいくつか置かれ
ていた。
どうすればいいのかわからなかったので、それらを
脇に寄せ、少しスペースを作った...。

seemed to spill out over the sides. Her nails, on both her fingers and her toes, were colored a bright pinkish-rose. Her hair was mostly a pale yellow, but right near her head it was a dark brown color. She must have been close to my mother's age.

After I finished the chips, we went inside and watched television. It had been a very long time since I had seen television. Charlie didn't come home until well past dark. He looked very tired, and not particularly happy to see me, but we did all sit together to eat the pizza in front of the television. From our limited conversation I figured that he had been working all day on a task that some other person had given him. We all watched the television for an hour before Charlie said he was going to bed. I was shown a room where I could sleep.

The bed in my room had stuffed animal toys on it. I wasn't sure what I should do with them, so I moved them off to the side and made a small space

16. 部屋には窓があったが、そこにはエアコンが取り付けられていた。
私は船の上で新鮮な空気をたっぷり浴びる生活に慣れていた。
安全で清潔な場所で休めることは嬉しかったが、その夜はあまり眠れなかった。
どうしても快適に感じられなかったのだ。

夜明け頃になってようやく眠りに落ちたようで、
目を覚ました時にはすでに遅く、チャーリーはもう出かけていた。
私は浴室を借りて身支度を整えた。
洗い流される感覚は心地よかったが、
彼女の可愛らしい石鹸や豪華なタオルを汚してしまうのではないかと気がかりだった。

昨夜食べたもののせいで喉がとても渇いており、
大きなグラスにたっぷりの水を飲み、再び歩き出したかった。
シンクのそばにグラスがあったので、水を汲もうとした。

「その水じゃダメよ！」と彼女が言った。
「ちょっと待って、ブリタの浄水を入れてあげるわ。
井戸水にはあらゆる種類の化学物質が含まれていて、EPAも…。

for myself. The room did have a window, but there was an air conditioner in it. I was used to lots of fresh air on the boat, and although I was happy to have a safe, clean place to rest, I didn't get much sleep that night. I just couldn't seem to get comfortable.

Around dawn I must have finally fallen asleep, and by the time I got up it was late, and Charlie was already gone. I used the bathroom to clean myself up, and it felt good to be washed, but I kept worrying that I was messing up her pretty little soaps and her fancy towels.

I was very thirsty from the food I had eaten the night before, and all I wanted was a big drink of water and to start walking once more. I saw the glasses over by the sink and began to help myself to some water.

"Not that water!" she said. "Here, let me get you something from the Britta. That well water is filled with all kinds of chemicals and the EPA or

17. EPAか何かが、この水は飲むなと言っていたわ。
それに、臭いもひどいのよ。」

彼女は冷蔵庫にあったプラスチックのピッチャーか
ら、私に飲み物を注いでくれた。

「本当に行かなくていいの、ハニー？
『デイズ・オブ・アワ・ライブズ』がちょうど始ま
るところよ。」

彼女の言葉の意味はよくわからなかったが、
私はもう滞在したくないことだけははっきりしてい
た。
彼女のもてなしに感謝を述べた後、
リュックを背負い、家を出て、ポーチを渡り、
階段を下り、車道へと向かった。

私はさらに六日間歩き続けた。
できるだけ小さな道を選び、
夜が来るたびに運を天に任せた。
車を避けるのは常に問題だった。
清潔な飲み水を確保するのも大変だった。
もちろん、快適に眠れる場所を見つけるのも難しか
った。
私はまだ健康で、体も強くなっていたが、
正直に言えば、幸せだとは言えなかった。
私がいるのは、不思議な国だった。

something like that told us not to drink it; besides, it smells bad."

She poured me a drink from a plastic pitcher that was in the refrigerator.

"Are you sure you don't want to stay honey? Days of Our Lives is just getting ready to come on."

I wasn't really sure what she meant, but I knew that I didn't want to stay. After thanking her for her hospitality, I lifted my pack and headed out the door, across the porch, down the steps, down the driveway, and along the road once more.

I walked for six more days, turning down smaller and smaller roads at every opportunity, and trusting my luck when night fell. Avoiding the cars was a constant problem, getting clean water to drink was a constant problem, and of course finding a comfortable place to sleep was a problem too. I was still healthy, and getting stronger, but if truth be told I could not say that I was happy. It was a strange land I was in.

18. 私の新しい計画である「最も小さな道を選ぶ」方
法は順調に進んでいた。
七日目の朝、私は美しい木々に囲まれた未舗装の道
を歩いていた。
これまでに通り過ぎた他の森とは異なり、
船から見た単一の種類の木だけの森とは違って、
この森には様々な種類の木々があり、
これまでこの国で見たどの木よりも大きかった。
道路沿いの雑草さえも、ここ数日間見てきたものと
は違って見えた。

道の両側では、多くの蝶が飛び交い、植物を訪れて
いた。
時折、リスやシカが私の前の道を横切った。
一度、カメを見かけたこともあった。
森の音もまた、これまでとはまるで違った。
木の上からは、さまざまな種類の鳥のさえずりが聞
こえてきた。
それらの鳴き声がどの鳥のものなのかはわからなか
ったが、
その美しい合唱を楽しんだ。

実際のところ、この日、私はついに心の中に喜びを
感じた。
背負っている荷物は軽くなったように感じ、
視界もここ数日間よりも澄んでいるようだった。
そして突然、ちょうどその時...。

My new plan to take the smallest roads was working out well. On the morning of the seventh day I was on a dirt road with beautiful trees all around. These were not like the other forests I had passed, like the ones I saw from the ship with only a single type of tree; this forest had many different types of trees, and the trees were bigger than any I had seen thus far in that country. Even the weeds along the roadside looked different from the ones I had been passing for days. There were numerous butterflies flitting back and forth across the road visiting the roadside plants. Occasionally I'd see a squirrel or a deer cross the road ahead of me. Once I saw a turtle. The sounds in this forest were much different too; songs from many different types of birds were coming from the treetops. I did not know the type of bird that any of the songs belonged too, but I enjoyed their chorus. In fact, for some reason, on that day I at last felt joy in my heart again. My pack felt lighter, and my vision seemed clearer than it had in the previous days. Suddenly, just when I

19. 永遠に歩き続けられるような気がしていたが、道
は突然終わった。

私は座ってしばらく休み、落ち着こうとしながら次
に何をすべきか考えた。
来た道を引き返すことを考えるのは嫌だった。
しかし、鳥の声に耳を傾け、美しい木々を眺めてい
ると、
道が終わった先に小道が続いているのに気がついた
。
そこには立ち入りを禁じる看板もなく、
小道は緩やかに丘を登り、最も大きな木々が立ち並
ぶ場所へと続いていた。
その木陰の道はとても魅力的に見えた。
少し休んだ後、私はその道を進むことを決めた。

その小道を歩き始めると、自分の中で何かが変わる
のを感じた。
百歩ほど進んだとき、私は自分がいる場所、そして
自分がしていることが正しいと確信した。
長い間抱いていた「この広大な国を歩いて旅する」
という考えは、
もう間違いではないと思えた。
私をこの方向へ導いた直感を再び信じることができ
た。
私は深い感動と、導いてくれる高次の力への感謝に
包まれた…。

felt as though I could walk forever, the road ended.

I sat and rested awhile, trying to remain calm as I thought about what I should do next. I dreaded the thought of retracing my steps. But as I sat there listening to the birds and looking at the beautiful trees, I noticed a path continuing on where the road had stopped. The path did not have any signs forbidding trespass, and the path looked very shady and inviting as it curved up a small rise and through an area containing the largest of the trees. After a brief rest I decided that I should follow that pathway.

It is difficult to describe the change that came over me as I walked along that path. After I had taken about a hundred steps, I suddenly felt a *rightness* in where I was and what I was doing. My idea, formulated so long ago, to walk through this large country no longer seemed to be a mistake. I could again trust the intuition that had led me in this direction. I was so overcome by emotion and thankfulness to the higher powers that guide the

20. 私は宇宙に導かれるようにリュックを下ろし、
膝をついて泣いた。
何が私の心境にこれほどの変化をもたらしたのかは
わからない。
たった一本の小道が、その理由になり得るだろうか
？
今になって思えば、それは私の内面で起こっていた
変化を
促す触媒のようなものだったのかもしれない。

私は感謝と絶望の両方に涙した。
自分のために、そして世界のために涙した。
私の血管を流れたすべての感情とともに泣いた。
涙が止んだとき、私は森の地面に落ちた湿った葉に
顔を押し付けていた。
その湿り気が自分の涙によるものなのか、
それとも森そのものの湿気なのかはわからなかった
。
まるで私と森がひとつの存在になったかのようだっ
た。

私たちの呼吸さえも共鳴していた。
私の吸う息は森の吐息から生まれ、
そして森は私の吐く息を吸い込んでいるように感じ
られた。
その甘い空気は私の体をめぐり、森を駆け抜け、
そして再び私のもとへと戻ってきた。
私は森とひとつになっていたのだ！

その瞬間、これまでに感じたことのないような
深い安らぎが私の全身を満たした。
私は泣き終え、静かに周囲を見渡し始めた…。

universe that I set down my pack, dropped to my knees, and cried. I cannot tell you what caused that extreme change in my condition. How could a small dirt path be responsible? I only imagine now that it was some sort of catalyst for a change that was happening inside of me all along.

I cried in gratefulness as well as despair; I cried for myself as well as for the world; I cried with every emotion that had ever run through my veins. At the end of my crying my face was pressed against the damp leaves on the forest floor. I don't know if the dampness came from my tears or from the forest itself. It was as if we had somehow become one thing. Even our breathing was mutual, I felt that my inhalations came from the forest's exhalations, and in turn the forest inhaled what I released. The sweet air was cycling through my being, then through the forest around me, and then returning once more to my body. I and the forest were one! And at that realization a calm unlike any other permeated my whole being. I was finished crying then, and I began to look around and to know the place where I sat.

21. 私は自分が座っているその場所を知っていると感
じた。

そこを訪れたことは一度もなかったはずなのに、
私は地球上のどの場所よりも、そこにいることに安
らぎを感じていた。
目にするものすべてが驚きと喜びを与えてくれた。
ふと見上げると、枝や葉の間から青い空が覗いてい
た。
なんて美しい模様なのだろう！
下を見ると、これまで気づいたことのない鮮やかな
緑の苔が広がっていた。
その柔らかさが目に焼き付いた。
白い花をつけた小さな植物もあった。
これまで見過ごしてきたものが、そこに存在してい
た。

私はじっと座り、動きたくなかった。
やがてさらに多くのものが私の意識に入ってきた。
小さな甲虫が私の手の上を登ってきたのだ。
顔の近くまで持ち上げてよく見ると、
それは私が今まで見た中で最も美しい甲虫だった。
この日、私が時間をともに過ごした植物や動物につ
いて語り続けることもできるが、
あなたもきっと、同じような森の中で、
このような心境になったことがあるのではないだろ
うか。

夜が訪れても、私はその場を離れることができなか
った。
その夜の眠りは…。

Although I had never been to that place before, I felt more at home there than I had at any other place on the planet. Every little thing I saw amazed and delighted me. I looked up and saw, far above, the blue pieces of sky between the branches and the leaves. What a lovely pattern they made! When I looked down I could see, as if for the first time, the moss, so bright green and soft! And a very small plant with white flowers - I had never noticed it before. I sat very still and did not want to move. Soon even more things came to my attention: a small beetle climbed on my hand; I drew it up to my face for a closer look and realized that it was the most beautiful beetle I had ever seen. I could go on and on and tell you about the other plants and animals I spent time with in appreciation that day, but you have probably been in such a forest, and in such a state of mind yourself.

Even when darkness fell I could not bring myself to leave that spot. My sleep that night was

22. それは、故郷を離れて以来、最も良い眠りだった
。
目を覚ますと、私はまだ周囲の美しい世界に畏敬の
念を抱いていた。
リュックを背負い、小道を進み続けた。
やがて、小さな澄んだ小川にたどり着いた。
私は喉が渇いており、その水に感謝しながら飲んだ
。
それは人生で最も純粋で甘美な水だった。

その日一日、小道を歩きながら、
前日に襲われた高揚した感覚がまだ残っていた。
森の中には、小さな青い実をつけた低木が点在して
いた。
私は試しにいくつか食べてみた。
甘かったので、有毒ではないだろうと判断した。
しばらくして、最初に食べた実が体に悪影響を及ぼ
さないことを確認すると、
私は次々と実を摘み、手いっぱいに集めて食べ始め
た。
ついに新鮮な果物を口にできたのだ！
何週間も果物なしで過ごした後、それを味わう喜び
は格別だった。
旅の途中で、リュックには他の食料もあったが、
そのどれも、この果実ほど美味しくは感じられなか
った。

森の二日目の終わりに、私は小道が次第に広くなっ
ていることに気づいた。
このあたりは、より頻繁に人が通る場所なのかもし
れない。

the best I had had since I left my homeland. When I woke I was still in awe of the beautiful world around me. I lifted my pack and continued down the trail; soon I came to a small clear stream. I was thirsty and grateful for a drink, and I can honestly tell you it was the purest, sweetest water I had ever had in my life. For the rest of the day, as I walked down that path, I retained something of the heightened state I had been struck by the day before. Bushes holding small blue berries were scattered throughout the forest. I tried some, and, as they were sweet, I doubted that they contained poison. After a time, when I noted that the first berries had not negatively affected me, I began to collect and eat them by the handful. Fresh fruit at last! After so many weeks without it I tasted it with a whole new appreciation. By that point in the journey I did have other food in my pack, but none of it tasted as good as those berries.

At the end of that second day in the forest I noticed that the path was becoming wider, as if it were more frequently traveled along this stretch.

23. 太陽がオレンジ色に染まり、地平線近くに沈もう
としていた頃、
私は小さな空き地に足を踏み入れた。
そこには鮮やかな赤い花が群生していた。
その花は特にこの光の中で美しかったが、
どこか場違いな印象を受けた。
しばらくそこで足を止めたが、日が暮れかけてきた
ため、
森の中の道を進みながら今夜のキャンプ地を探し続
けた。

数百ヤード進んだところで、道は突然広い草地へと
開けた。
薄明かりの中で、遠くに薄い色の動物が草を食んで
いるのがかすかに見えた。
彼らは私の存在を気にする様子もなかった。
やがて私は柵があることに気づき、
彼らが家畜であることを理解した。
しかし、こんなにも辺鄙な場所に、一体誰が住んで
いるというのだろうか？

牧草地の外側を、柵に沿って歩き続けた。
暗闇がすぐそこまで迫っていた。
森へ戻って野営することを考え始めたそのとき、
突然犬の吠える声が聞こえた。
最初は恐怖を感じたが、その犬が私を攻撃するつも
りではないことに気づいた。
建物の中に私は...。

When the sun turned orange, low on the horizon, I walked into a small clearing that contained a patch of bright red flowers. Although the flowers were beautiful, especially in that light, there was something about them that made them seem out of place. I hesitated there for a while, and when it was getting close to dark I continued along the forested path in search of a campsite for the evening. In a few hundred yards the path suddenly opened onto a large clearing. In the dusky light I could just barely see light colored animals grazing in the distance. They did not seem alarmed by my presence. Eventually I saw that there was a fence; I realized that they must be domestic animals. But who on God's green Earth would live way out here, I wondered.

I walked around the outside edge of the pasture, guided by the fence, as darkness was falling fast. I was considering walking back into the woods to camp when suddenly a dog started barking. At first I was very frightened, but then I saw that the dog did not mean to attack me. In a building I had

24. 影になっていて気づかなかったが、突然明かりが
灯った。
ドアが開き、一人の女性が姿を現し、私に声をかけ
た。
「そこにいるのは誰？」と彼女は尋ねた。
私はどもりながら、
自分が何者で、なぜここにいるのかを短い言葉で説
明しようとした。
しかし、犬が吠え続ける中で説明するのは特に難し
かった。
私の理由と、今夜眠る場所が必要だということを伝
えようとしたが、
状況はますます気まずくなっていった。

「いい子ね、トビー。もう静かにして。」
そう言った後、彼女は私に向かって言った。
「あなたのことをよく知るまでは、家の中では眠ら
せられないわ。
ここで待っていて。」

彼女は家の中へ戻り、
しばらくすると古びたウールの毛布を持って出てき
た。
「ついてきて。」

もうすっかり暗くなっていたが、
彼女はまるで昼間のように迷いなく歩いていた。
私たちは牧草地の柵に沿って反対側へ進んだ。
彼女は門を開き、私を小さな納屋のような建物へと
導いた。
その建物は、牧草地に向かって開かれた前面と、
閉ざされた奥側を持っていた…。

not noticed, because it was in the shadows, a light came on. A woman stepped out of the door and addressed me.

"Who's out there?" she asked.

I stammered, not knowing quite how to explain who I was and what I was doing there in a few short words. It made things especially awkward that the dog continued to bark while I tried to explain my reason for being there and my need for a place to sleep.

"Good dog Toby, hush now," said the woman, and then to me: "You can't sleep inside until I know you better, wait here."

The woman went back into the house and came out with an old wool blanket.

"Follow me," she said.

Although it was already dark she walked as if it were bright as day. We followed the pasture fence around to the opposite side. She opened a gate and led me toward a small shed-like building; open in the front, toward the pasture, and closed in the back,

25. 建物の奥側には柵があり、開放された納屋の一区画には、
干し草の俵が積まれていた。
女性はその干し草の上に毛布を広げ、私の方を向いて言った。

「ここで快適に過ごせるといいけれど。
よかったら、朝になったらドアをノックしてね。」

そう言い残し、彼女は家の方へと歩き去っていった。

彼女が去った後、辺りはとても、とても静かになった。
耳の中で血液の流れる音さえ聞こえるほどだった。
旅の中で、私は多くの奇妙な状況に慣れ、
自分はどんな環境にも適応できると考えていた。
しかし、その夜の状況は私にとって完全に予想外だった。
眠気を感じるどころか、突然体がエネルギーに満ちたように感じた。

ウールの毛布の上に横になる準備をしたが、
自分が落ち着いて眠れるまでには何時間もかかることがわかっていた。

「ここは一体どこなのだろう？」
そう思いながら、私は静かに休んでいた…。

toward the fence. One bay of the open shed was filled with bales of straw. The woman spread out the blanket over the bales and turned to me.

"I hope you're comfortable here. If you like, in the morning, you can knock on the door."

With those words she turned and walked back toward the house.

After she left it became very, very quiet and I could hear the blood rushing through my ears. In all my journeys I had become used to strange new circumstances, and considered myself extremely flexible, but for some reason the circumstances of that evening took me utterly by surprise. Instead of feeling sleepy I suddenly felt charged with energy. I arranged myself for sleeping on the woolen blanket, but I knew that it would be hours before I was calm enough to sleep.

Where was I? I wondered. As I rested after

26. 長い一日が終わり、呼吸がようやく落ち着いたとき、
私はついに自分の周囲をじっくりと味わうことができた。
私の下に敷かれた干し草の俵は、甘く清らかな香りを放っていた。
横になったまま、開け放たれた納屋の側から星を眺めることができた。
それは美しく、静かで、きらめく夜だった。
私は船上での時間を思い出した。
ここでも同じような、新鮮で安全な感覚を抱いていた。
私は長い間、空を見つめ続けた。
最後に星を心から感謝して眺めたのはいつだっただろうか、と考えた。
あの星の一つ一つが、私たちの太陽と同じように、無数の生命を育んでいるのかもしれない。
もしかすると、今、この瞬間、
誰かが私の星の光を眺めているのだろうか？
そもそも「今」とは何なのだろう？
私の目に届くまでに、あの光はどれほどの時間を旅してきたのか？
そのとき、空に閃光が走った。
一瞬、息をのんだが、すぐに頭の中で言葉が浮かんだ。「流れ星だ。」
その後も、次の一時間の間にいくつかの流れ星が見えたが、
やがて私は眠りについた。
夜中、一度目を覚ました。
それは、それまで聞こえなかった音に気づいたからだった。
私は耳を澄ませ、その正体を探ろうとした…

the long day, and my breathing slowed at last, I could finally appreciate my surroundings. The bales beneath me were giving off the sweet, clean, smell of straw. From where I lay I could see stars out of the open side of the shed. It was a beautiful, quiet, sparkling evening. I thought back to my time on board the ship. I felt something like that same fresh, safe feeling here. I stared at the sky for a long time. How long had it been since I really appreciated the stars, I wondered. Each one of those stars could support multitudes of living things, as our star does. Could they be looking at the light from my star now? And what is *now* anyway? How long ago had that light started its journey toward my eyes?

Then in a flash a bright line streaked through the sky. It took my breath for a split second until my mind found the words: shooting star. There were a few more during the next hour, but after that I dozed off. I woke once during the night, aroused by a sound that had not been there earlier. I had to listen closely before I realized that

27. 雨の音が静かに納屋の屋根を打っていた。
雨をしのげることに感謝しながらも、
不思議なことに、まだ星が明るく輝いているのが見
えた。
それはまるで珍しい天気雨のようだった。
太陽が輝いているのに雨が降る、その異様さの中に
魔法のような喜びがある。
その夜、私は流星群を目の当たりにし、
小さな雨粒を通して星を見つめる練習をした。

その夜、最も奇妙な考えが私の心をよぎった。
横になりながら、これからの人生の後半では、
もっと創造的なことに時間を使いたいと願った。
絵を学ぶべきかもしれないし、
楽器を演奏できるようになりたいとも思った。
あるいは、少なくとも旅の物語を文章に残しておく
べきかもしれない、と。

雨は空気に素晴らしい涼しさをもたらした。
木々や草花が、その葉を洗い流され、根が潤うこと
を喜んでいるのがわかった。
そして、私もまたその中で幸せを感じていた。
私が横になっている場所は森の中ではなかったが、
周囲に森の存在を強く感じることができた。

the sound was a gentle rain hitting the shed roof. I was glad to be protected from the rain, but strangely enough I could still see the stars shining brightly. It must have been like a rare *sun shower*; when the sun is shining, yet it is raining, and there is a magical delight in the unusualness of it. That night I was witness to a *star shower* and I practiced seeing the stars through the small falling drops.

The most unusual thoughts kept me company that night. I hoped, as I lay there, that in the next half of my life I could spend more time being creative. I decided that I should learn to paint, or play a musical instrument, or at least write down some of the stories from my travels.

The rain brought a wonderful coolness to the air. I knew that the trees and other plants were happy to have their leaves washed and their roots dampened. And I was happy in their midst, for although the spot where I laid was not forested, I could feel the presence of the forest all around me. I

28. 私は再び穏やかな雨音を聞きながら眠りに落ちた
。

最初の陽の光が木々を通り抜け、
雄鶏が朝の訪れを告げる鳴き声を上げたとき、私は
目を覚ました。
驚いたことに、ほんの数十センチ先に、
三匹の大きな動物がじっと私を見つめていた。
最初は、それらの生き物を恐れるべきかどうかわか
らなかった。
しかし、彼らはそれほど威圧的には見えなかった。
恐れる必要はないと判断し、
さらに動物は恐怖を感じ取ることがあると聞いたこ
とがあったので、
私は意識的に心を落ち着けることにした。
急な動きをしないように注意し、
静かで親しみやすい声で彼らに話しかけ始めた。

それらの動物は羊だった。
私がリラックスすると、彼らも同じように落ち着い
た。
羊の目をじっくりと見つめたことはこれまでなかっ
たが、
こうして横になりながら、彼らが私をじっと見つめ
ることで、
完璧な機会が訪れた。
彼らの目が、神経を通じて脳へ映像を伝えているこ
とを考えると、
私の目と同じ仕組みなのだと実感し、不思議な気持
ちになった。
私は考えた…。

drifted off to sleep again listening to the gentle rain.

I woke when the first rays of sunlight came through the trees, and a rooster called out a greeting to it. I was startled to see three large animals just a foot or two away and watching me intently. At first I didn't know if I should be frightened of the creatures or not. They didn't look too menacing, so I decided that fear was unnecessary, and, besides I had heard that some animals were able to sense it, so I consciously brought my mind to a calmer place, I tried not to move too rapidly, and I began to talk to the animals in a quiet, friendly, tone of voice.

The animals were sheep, and I could see that as I relaxed, they relaxed too. I had never looked deeply into a sheep's eyes before, but lying there, with them looking at me like that, I had the perfect opportunity. It was fascinating to think that their eyes were transmitting the scene through nerves to their brains the same as mine were. I wondered

29. 私たちは他に何を共有しているのだろう。
どんな思考を、どんな感情を…。

羊たちと目覚めるのはとても興味深い体験だったが、
膀胱がいっぱいで、そろそろ起きなければならなかった。
私は荷物をまとめ、昨夜通った門から牧草地を出た。
羊たちは私についてきたが、門を閉めるとその場にとどまる様子だった。

牧草地の反対側には、昨夜は影に隠れていた家が見えた。
私は森の中へ入り、用を足しながら考えた。
このまま歩き続けるべきだろうか？
あのコテージの扉を叩く義務はないと感じていた。
毛布も、彼女が置いた場所から自分で回収できるだろう。

確かに、私の食料は少なくなっていた。
だが、私を引き返させたのは食料ではなかった。
この場所には、私が学ぶべき何かがある。
この広大な国の中で、なぜ私はこの道へと導かれたのか？

そう思った私は、再び引き返した。
まずは羊たちの元へ戻り、毛布を払い畳んだ。
そして、確かな足取りで、コテージの扉へと向かった。

what else we shared, what thoughts, what feelings.

Waking up to sheep was very interesting, but my bladder was full, and it was time to rise. I packed up my things and left the pasture through the gate we had come in the night before. The sheep followed me to the gate, but seemed willing to stay when I closed it behind me. Around the other side of the pasture I could see the house that had been in the shadows the previous evening. I walked into the woods to relieve the pressure in my bladder, and I wondered if I should just keep going. I felt no obligation to return and knock on that cottage door. The owner would certainly be able to retrieve the blanket from where she put it. True, my food supplies were low, but I tell you it wasn't the food that made me turn and head back. There was some lesson there for me I was sure, some reason why, in that huge country, I had been led down that particular path. So I did turn back, first back to my friends the sheep, to shake out and fold the blanket, and then in sure steps toward the door of the cottage.

30.「毛布を返してくれてありがとう。」
彼女はドアを開けるとそう言った。
「グレンダ、グラディス、グレーテルにはもう会ったでしょう？
私はただの、木を愛する女よ。」

そう言いながら、彼女は手を差し出した。
私が握手をすると、彼女は朝食に招待してくれた。
空気中に漂う香ばしい香りに、断ることなど考えられなかった。
朝食は、新鮮なスクランブルエッグと炒めた玉ねぎ
、
それに野生のキノコが添えられていた。
飲み物はミントティーだった。

彼女の息子、ジャスティンも一緒に朝食をとった。
彼は12歳くらいに見えた。
明るく快活な少年で、私や私の旅に対して強い好奇心を持っていた。
母と息子の二人とも、健康的な輝きを放っていた。
母親はほっそりとしており、髪が白髪交じりになっているのがわかった。
彼らの服装はシンプルで、綿のシャツとズボンを身につけ、
二人とも裸足だった。

彼らは、プラスチック屋根のレストランにいた人々や、
この旅で出会った他の人々とはまったく違って見えた。
だが、私はその違いが何なのか、はっきりとはわからなかった。

"Thank you for returning the blanket, she said after she opened the door. "I assume you met Glenda, Gladys, and Gretel already, and me -- I'm just a woman who loves trees." And with those words she held out her hand for me to shake.

She invited me in for breakfast and the aroma in the air was mouthwatering. I couldn't think of refusing. Breakfast was fresh scrambled eggs with cooked onions and wild mushrooms. We had mint tea to drink. The woman's son, Justin, ate with us too. He looked to be about twelve years old. A bright and sunny boy full of curiosity about me and my travels. Both mother and son had a healthy glow about them. The mother was slender, and I could see that her hair was graying. Their clothes were simple, cotton shirts and pants, and both were barefoot. They looked very different from the people in the plastic-roofed restaurants, and the rest of the people I had met on this part of the journey, although I couldn't quite figure out what the difference was.

31. 朝食の後に粘土を掘るつもりよ。」
彼女はそう言った。
「手伝ってくれると助かるわ。」

私は、宿と美味しい朝食の代わりに作業を手伝うの
は公平な取引だと思い、同意した。

彼女と息子が皿を片付け、朝食の食器を洗っている
間、
私は部屋を見回す時間があった。
それはシンプルな空間だった。
開放された木製の棚が並び、
さまざまなものが入った瓶が置かれていた。
いくつかの瓶にはフルーツジャムが、
他の瓶には乾燥した豆が、
そしてさらに別の瓶には乾燥した葉のようなものが
入っていた。
おそらく、何らかの薬草だろう。

この部屋はシンプルで実用的だったが、
美しさや芸術性を忘れてはいなかった。
テーブルの中央には陶器の花瓶があり、
私がここへ来る途中に見たのと同じ赤い花が生けら
れていた。
窓にはシンプルなカーテンが掛けられ、
そのうちの一つの窓の中心には小さなステンドグラ
スのパネルが吊るされていた。

その部屋は、私にとってとても居心地の良い空間だ
った。

"After breakfast I'm going to dig some clay," she said. "I sure could use help."

I agreed that helping with a chore was a fair trade for a place to sleep and a wonderful breakfast. As the two cleared the plates and washed the breakfast dishes, I had time to look around the room. It was a simple place, with rows of open wooden shelves holding jars filled with all sorts of things. In some of the jars were fruit preserves, in others there were dried beans, and still other jars contained what looked like dried leaves - probably herbs of some sort. Although the room was simple and functional it did not neglect beauty or art. In the middle of the table was a stoneware vase holding the same type of red flowers I had seen on my way in. The simple windows were curtained, and hanging in the center of one window was a small stained-glass panel. It was a room I felt very comfortable in.

32. 二人が後片付けを終えると、
彼女と少年はドアのそばのベンチに座り、ブーツを
履いた。

「ジャスティン、今朝は女の子たちの世話をして、
それから卵を集めておいてくれる？」

「わかったよ、ママ。」
少年はそう答えた。

それ以上の会話もなく、
二人はそれぞれの目的地へと歩き出した。
少年は牧草地へ、
女性は私が昨晩来た道とは違う小道へと進んでいっ
た。
私は彼女の後ろについて行った。

しばらく歩くと、小さな小川にたどり着いた。
荷物を背負わずに歩くのはとても気持ちがよかった
ので、
この距離を歩くことはまったく苦にならなかった。
しかし、小道は小川で終わっていた。
だが、私たちの目的地はまだ先だった。

女性は川の中の岩から岩へと飛び移りながら、
上流へと進み始めた。
当然のように、私もそれに続いた。
時には、大きく跳躍しなければならない場面もあっ
たが、
彼女がそんな動きを難なくこなしていることに、
私は少し驚いた...。

After they finished cleaning up, the two sat on a bench by the door to put on their boots.

"Justin," she said, "can you take care of the girls this morning, and collect the eggs while we get the clay?

"No problem, mom," he replied.

Without further discussion they both headed out the door, the boy toward the pasture, and the woman toward a different path than the one I had come in on. I followed along behind her. We walked for a good while before we came to a small creek; I didn't mind the walk since it felt very nice to walk without wearing my pack. The trail ended at the creek, but we were not yet at our destination. The woman proceeded up the creek by stepping from rock to rock; of course I continued to follow. At times we had to leap to reach the next rock, and I was faintly surprised to see that she could leap as

33.「ここよ。」
彼女はそう言って、小川沿いの小さな隆起のような
場所にしゃがみ込んだ。
「粘土よ。」

立ち止まったことで、私は改めて周囲を見渡した。
巨大な木々に囲まれていたが、それぞれの間には十
分な空間があった。
そのため、暗く閉ざされた雰囲気ではなく、
むしろ開放的な森に感じられた。
森の床には、光の斑点が美しい抽象模様を描いてい
た。
場所によっては、まるで光の筋が空気を通り抜けて
いるのが見えるようだった。

光の筋の中には、小さな虫たちが浮かび、照らし出
されていた。
森の中央を流れるのは、私たちがたどってきた小川
だった。
そして、光を見る感覚を学んだことで、
水の中にまで光が差し込み、
川底の色とりどりの小さな石たちを照らし出してい
るのがわかった。

ここはただの場所ではなかった。
岩の上に座り、ただ眺めているだけでも、
どれほどの時間が経ってしまうのだろうか…。

far as I could.

"Here we are," she said, and squatted down next to what looked like a small rise along the stream. "Clay."

Now that we had stopped, I looked around at where I was. Giant trees surrounded us, but there was plenty of space between them. Instead of feeling dark and closed in, this forest felt very open. There were flecks of light in a beautiful abstract pattern hitting the forest floor. In some places it was as if you could actually see the beams of light coming through the air. In the air were a few tiny insects that were illuminated by the light beams. Running through the center of the forest was the stream we had followed, and once I learned how to see the light in this way, I could see places where the light was penetrating the water and illuminating the small multi-hued rocks on the stream's bottom. This is just a brief description of the place. I could have sat on a rock and looked

34. 何時間でもここに座って眺めていたかったが、
彼女は明らかにやるべきことを決めていた。

「あれはブナの木よ。」
彼女はそう言った。
「ブナも粘土が好きなの。
スコップを持ってきたけど、私は普段、手で掘るの
よ。」

そう言いながら、彼女は肩に掛けた袋から防水の袋
を取り出し、私に渡した。
彼女は粘土を袋に詰める作業を始め、私はそれを見
ながら同じようにやってみた。
作業は単純だった。
土手から手で粘土を掘り出し、袋に入れるだけ。
粘土は滑りやすく、淡い青みがかった灰色をしてお
り、
掘った跡に指の形が残るのがわかった。
その感触は独特だったが、不快ではなかった。
彼女は、「持てる分だけ掘るように」と忠告した。

作業を終えた後、私は掘った跡のことなど考えもし
なかったが、
彼女は石を水で濡らし、
その跡をなでるようにして滑らかにしていた。
跡が残らないように元の状態に戻していた…

around for hours, but the woman obviously had her task in mind.

"Those are beech trees," she said, "they like the clay too. I brought a trowel you can use if you want to, but I usually just use my hands."

With that remark she handed me a waterproof sack from the bag slung over her shoulder. She worked at filling her sack and I watched and tried to follow what she was doing. The job was fairly simple, digging handfuls of clay out of the bank and putting them in the sack. The clay was slippery, a light bluish-gray color, and you could see impressions in it from where your fingers had dug. It was an unusual sensation, but it wasn't unpleasant. She warned me to only dig as much as I could carry.

When we had finished I didn't give a thought to the marks we made in the bank, but she wet a stone and rubbed it over the area, smoothing out the impressions and leaving it looking close to

35. 私たちは流れる小川で手を洗った。
水は冷たかった！
私はズボンで手を拭き、その後、手を見下ろした。
こんなに手がきれいになったのは初めてかもしれない。
粘土が爪の間や皮膚の小さな隙間まで洗い流していた。
まるで赤ん坊の手のように、新しく見えた。

私は驚いた。
「土」が人をきれいにすることができるとは！
そして、その瞬間、私は初めて気づいた。
「手」というものが、なんと驚くべき器官なのかと
。
これまで私は、クジャクの羽の美しさや、
動物の毛並みの柔らかさ、
あるいは象の鼻の不思議な機能性には感嘆してきた
。
しかし、人間の手に対して驚嘆することは、
これまでなかったのかもしれない。

突然、私は体全体を手と同じように清潔にしたくなった。
そこで彼女に尋ねた。
「ここで体を洗ってもいいですか？」

「もちろんよ。」
彼女はそう答えた。

私は、彼女がその場を離れるか、
せめて少し森の中へ移動して私にプライバシーを与えるものと期待していた。
しかし、彼女はその場から動かなかった。
私は考えた…。

the way we found it. We washed off our hands in the running stream - the water was cold! I dried my hands on my pants and then looked down at them. I don't think my hands had ever been so clean. The clay had cleaned out under my nails and every little fold of my skin. My hands looked almost new to me, like a baby's. I marveled at how 'dirt' could actually make one cleaner, and I saw, as if for the first time, what miraculous objects these things called 'hands' were. I had, in the past, admired the incredible beauty of peacock feathers, or the amazing softness of an animal's fur, or even the strange functionality of an elephant's trunk; but I had forgotten, or never remembered, to marvel at human hands.

Suddenly I wanted the rest of my body to be as clean as my hands. I asked the woman if I could bathe there in the stream.

"Certainly," she replied.

I expected her to head back, or at least to walk into the woods a bit to give me privacy, but she stayed right where she was. When I think about

36. 今になって考えると、
出会ったばかりの女性の前で服を脱いだのは少し奇妙なことかもしれない。
しかし、その時はそれがまったく自然なことに思えた。

小川は浅かったので、体全体を水に浸すためには、
川底の砂利の上に横たわる必要があった。
なんと素晴らしく冷たい感触だろう！
息をのむような心地よさだった。
水が髪を流れ、顔を伝い、
体のすべてを包み込んでいった。

私は見上げた。
木々の梢が小川の上で交わっていた。
その瞬間、まるで私の意識が体を離れ、
木々の高みに昇っていくように感じた。
しかし、すぐに意識は冷たい水の中の体へと戻った。

水から出たとき、
これまでにないほど清々しい気持ちだった。
まるで、過去一週間の悩みや疲れが、
水と共に流れていったかのようだった。

女性は微笑みを浮かべながら、森を眺めていた。
「プロトノタリー・ワーブラーよ。」
彼女はそう言った。
「聞こえる？」

it now, I find it unusual that I removed my clothes in front of a woman I had just met, but at the time it seemed perfectly natural.

The stream was shallow, so to submerge my entire body I had to lie flat on the gravel in the streambed. What a marvelous cool sensation it was! Almost breathtaking! The water ran through my hair and over my face and down the length of my body. I was looking up at the tops of the trees meeting over the stream. For a few moments it was as if my awareness had left my body and was high up in the trees, but soon I was back in my body in the cold stream. When I stepped out of that water I felt like I had never been cleaner. It was as if all the worries and cares of the previous week had flowed down the stream with the water.

The woman just sat looking into the forest with a small smile on her face. "Prothonotary warbler," she said, "do you hear it?"

37. 私の洗いたての耳は、澄んだ鳥の声をはっきりと
聞き取ることができた。

女性は食べ物を持ってきており、
私は岩の上で乾かしながら、それを分けてもらった
。
突然、私は彼女のことをもっと知りたくなり、
同時に、私のことも彼女に知ってほしいと思った。

まず、私は彼女の息子がとても好きだと伝え、
それから彼女の娘たちについて尋ねた。

「私の娘？」

今朝、彼女がジャスティンに「女の子たちの世話を
お願い」と言っていたことを話した。

「ああ、女の子たちね。」
彼女は笑った。

そして、その笑い声は彼女を若々しく輝かせた。
彼女は決して若い女性ではなかったが、
その笑顔には、私が常に「若さ」と結びつけて考え
るような喜びが満ちていた。

「女の子たちっていうのはね、私の羊たちのことよ
。
グレンダ、グラディス、それから...」

And my freshly washed ears could hear the
clear notes.

The woman had brought some food, and as I
sat drying on the rock she shared it with me.
Suddenly I wanted to know all about her and I
wanted her to know all about me. I started by telling
her that I liked her son very much, and I asked about
her daughters.

"My daughters?"

This morning, I told her, she had asked Justin
to take care of the girls. "Ohh the girls," she
laughed.

And although she was certainly not a young
woman, when she laughed she was filled with a
joyousness that I have always associated with youth.

"The girls are my sheep: Glenda, Gladys and

38. グレーテル。」

そして、私も笑い出した。
その笑い声を、さえずる鳥が聞き、鳥もまた笑い声
で応えた。

「ジャスティンが、女の子たちの乳を搾るのよ。」
彼女はそう言った。
「戻ったら、ヨーグルトを作るわ。
きっと羊のミルクのヨーグルトなんて食べたことな
いでしょ？
すごく美味しいのよ。
あなたも残って試してみたらどう？
私の蜂蜜もかけてあげるわよ。」

私はすでに、この夜もここに泊まることを決めてい
た。
地球上のどこよりも、ここにいたかった。
しかし、それを口にすることはなかった。
ヨーグルトができるまでいよう、という素振りさえ
見せなかった。
その代わりに、私は彼女の息子について尋ねた。
なぜ彼は学校に行っていないのか、と。

「昔、一度だけその学校を訪れたことがあるの。」
彼女はそう言った。
「森についての授業をしてほしいと頼まれたのよ。
あれは何年も前のこと。
あの時の子どもたちは...」

Gretel."

And then I started laughing too. And our laughter was heard by the warbler, and it laughed back.

"Justin's going to milk the girls," she said, "and when we get back I'll make some yogurt. I bet you've never had sheep's milk yogurt - it's delicious - you should stay and try some. I'll even put some of my honey on it for you."

Already I knew that I would be staying the night there again. I had no desire to be any place else on Earth. But I didn't say that, or even hint that I might stay long enough for some yogurt. Instead, I asked about her son and why he wasn't in school.

"I visited that school once," she said. "They asked me to teach a class about the forest. That was a number of years ago, and the children there, who

39. 彼らは今のジャスティンと同じくらいの年齢だっ
たけど、
森について何も知らなかったの。
どの植物が毒で、どの植物が食べられるかもわから
ない。
どの蛇が卵を産み、どの蛇が子を直接産むのかも知
らない。
それに、カエデとオークの違いさえわからなかった
のよ！」

「その日、私は決めたの。
学校は、私が息子に学んでほしいことを教えていな
いって。
だったら、どうして彼を一日中建物の中に閉じ込め
て、
他の人たちが教えたいことを学ばせなきゃならない
の？

私たちの社会は、これまでになく高い教育を受けて
いる。
でも、環境を破壊する速度も、これまでになく速く
なっている。
そんなの、何のための教育なのかしら？」

彼女は怒りや恨みを込めて言ったのではなかった。
ただ、誰もが知っている事実を淡々と述べているよ
うだった。

彼女は私の方を向き、まっすぐ私の目を見つめた。
そして、初めて私は、彼女の瞳の本当の青さを見た
。

were about the age Justin is now, didn't know a thing about the forest. They didn't know which plants would poison you, and which would fill you up; they didn't know which snakes lay eggs and which ones give birth to live young; why they couldn't even tell an oak from a maple!"

"I decided that very day that the schools weren't teaching the things I wanted my son to learn. So why should I make him sit inside a building all day to learn the things other people want him to learn? Our population is more educated than ever before, but they're also destroying the environment at a faster pace than ever before. What kind of education is that?"

She didn't say it with anger or malice, she said it simply as though she were just stating a common fact.

She turned toward me and looked me directly in the eyes, and for the first time I could see their true blueness.

40.「あなたにとって、この世界で最も大切なものは
二つ何？」
彼女はそう尋ねた。

私は一瞬考えた。
彼女が私に興味を持ってくれたことが、密かに嬉し
かった。

「冒険と富だ。」
私は答えた。
「世界を見て回りたいし、そのための手段を手に入
れたい。」

「私にとって最も大切なものは、息子とこの森よ。
」
彼女は言った。
「ある意味では、この二つは同じものなの。
この森がなければ、私の息子は今とは全く違う人間
に育つでしょう。
もしかしたら、この森がなければ、
彼もお金と冒険を最高の目標にするような人間にな
ってしまうかもしれないわね。」

彼女の言葉に傷つく暇もなかった。
なぜなら、その言葉と同時に、彼女は私に触れたか
らだ。
その手の感触には、思いやりと理解が込められてい
た。
まるで彼女に祝福されているかのように感じた。

「私はね、自分の手を使って働くことに、
本当に大きな喜びを感じるのよ...

"What are the two most important things in the world to you?" she asked.

I paused for a moment, secretly pleased that she wanted to know about me. "Adventure and wealth," I told her. "I want to see the world and to have the means to do so."

"Well, the two most important things to me are my son and this forest," she said. "In some ways they are one and the same. Without this forest surrounding him my son would grow to be a very different man than the one I see him becoming now. Perhaps without this forest he would turn out to be a man with money and adventure as his highest goals."

I didn't have time to be hurt by her remark, because as she made it she touched me. Her touch was one of compassion and understanding. I felt as though I were being blessed by her in some way.

"I get a lot of pleasure from working my

41. 私は小さな農場を営みながら、陶芸をしているの
。
蜂蜜のためのミツバチ、卵を産む鶏、
チーズを作るための羊のミルクがあるわ。
それに、さまざまな花やハーブ、野菜を育てている
。
でも、正直に言うと、
それらはただ私が生きて健康でいるためのものにす
ぎないの。
本当に大切な仕事は、この森を守ることよ。

しばらくの間、私たちは沈黙していた。
そして、彼女は再び話し始めた。

「ここにある木々が、他の場所で見たものよりも大
きいことに気づいた？」
これを維持するには、たくさんの希望と努力が必要
だったのよ。
この森は何度も伐採の危機にさらされたけれど、
私は決して彼らに好き勝手させなかった。
この森は一度も伐採されたことがない。
だからこそ、特別な存在感を持っているのを感じら
れるでしょう？

私は、初めてこの森に足を踏み入れたときの体験を
彼女に話してはいなかった。
しかし、彼女の言葉を聞きながら、
私はその時のことを思い出していた。

「私は、この森を守るために、できる限りのことを
するつもりよ…」

small farm and making my pottery. I have bees for honey and chickens for eggs, and sheep's milk for cheese; I grow many different kinds of flowers, herbs, and vegetables; but to be honest, all of that is just to keep me alive and healthy while I do my real work - which is protecting this forest."

We were both quiet for a time before she continued.

"You must have noticed that the trees here are larger than you've seen in other places? It took lots of hopefulness and hard work to keep them that way. This forest has been under assault numerous times, but I never let them get away with cutting it. This forest has *never* been cut, and you can feel that it possesses a special dimension because of that."

I had not told her about my experience that first day in the forest, but I was thinking of it as she spoke.

"I will do all in my power to prevent this

42.「私はこの森が伐採されるのを全力で阻止するつ
もりよ。
なぜなら、もし伐採されてしまえば、
ここにある特別な何かが失われてしまうと分かって
いるから。」

「いわゆる林業者たちは、
いつも『再植林する』『持続可能な伐採を行う』と
言うわ。
でも、私の考える本当の持続可能性とは、
この森が続くこと、永遠に存続することなの。
私の生涯の間も、私の息子の世代にも、
そして未来のすべての世代にわたって続いていくこ
と。
もしかしたら、私の言葉はありふれたスローガンの
ように聞こえるかもしれない。
でも、私は心からそう信じているのよ。」

私は、彼女の言葉が本心からのものであると分かっ
た。
彼女は心の底から語っていた。

「どれだけ私が時間と心、魂を森に捧げても、
森はそれ以上のものを私に返してくれるの。
例えば、私のきれいな水の源である泉は、
完全にこの森に依存しているのよ。
もし森が伐採されてしまえば、泉は枯れ、
私はこの場所を離れざるを得なくなる。
でも、私はどこへ行けばいいの？」

私は、井戸を掘ることを提案した。

forest from being cut, because I know that if it is then something very special will be lost. The so-called foresters always say they will replant, that they will harvest sustainably; but my vision is for true sustainability, meaning that this forest will sustain - will go on indefinitely - for my lifetime and my son's and for all generations to come. I know that my words might sound like sappy slogans to you, but I mean them with all my heart."

And I did know that she meant them. I could feel that she was speaking from her heart.

"No matter how much I give of my time and my heart and my soul to the forest, she gives me even more back. For example, the spring, source of my clean water, is totally dependent on this forest. If the forest were cleared my spring would dry up and I would have to leave this place. Where would I go?"

I suggested that she might be able to drill a well.

43. 「私たちの帯水層には毒素が含まれているのよ。
」
彼女は言った。
「私はそんな水を自分の体に入れたり、
息子に飲ませたりすることはできない。
羊にさえも与えたくないの。
私は彼女たちをとても大切に思っているし、
それに化学物質の多くは羊のミルクに入り、
やがてはチーズに、そして私たちの体に入ってしま
うから。

たとえ、ボトルウォーターやフィルターで対応でき
ると言われても、
動物たちはどうすればいいの？
野生の動物たちは？
あの小さな鳥は何を飲めばいいの？
どこに巣を作ればいいの？
いいえ、この森は植え直すことはできない。
守らなければならないのよ。」

そして、私は夢から覚めた。
そこは、川をさかのぼりながら港へ向かう帆船のデ
ッキだった。
私は誓った。
再びこの愛しい大地に足を踏み入れたとき、
私は全力を尽くして森を守ると。

そして、それがまさに今日まで私がやり続けてきた
ことなの。

終わり

"Our aquifer contains toxins," she said. "I will not put that water in my body or give it to my son. I will not even feed it to my sheep. I care for them too much, and besides many of the chemicals would enter their milk, and then my cheese, and then our bodies. Even if, as some say, I could buy bottled water or filters, what will the animals do? The wild animals I mean. What will the warbler drink? Where will she nest? No, the forest cannot be replanted, it must be saved."

And then I woke from the dream, and there I was lying on the deck of the sailboat headed up the river toward the dock. I swore that when my feet touched that sweet earth again, I would do all in my power to protect her forests. And that is exactly what I have been doing, right up until this very day.

The End

Afterword

I wrote this parable in the early 2000's. From the beginning, I imagined it in Japanese on one side of the page and English on the other. However I didn't know anyone skilled in the Japanese language, so I never had it translated. But I never forgot about my beloved parable, and I kept thinking that someday a Japanese translator would appear in my world. Besides, I got very, very busy writing about forests and working to save them.

This year, after twenty years of waiting, a translator did appear... in the following pages my original English was translated into Kanji by AI.

If you are a Japanese translator and would like to comment on it, or help improve it, please email me: joan@oldgrowthforest.net.

If you, too, want to help save old-growth forests, or just visit them, please explore the webpage www.OldGrowthForest.net.